THE
MAGIC
SWORD

There are lots of Early Reader
stories you might enjoy.

Look at the back of the book,
or for a complete list, visit
www.orionchildrensbooks.com

THE MAGIC SWORD

Written and illustrated by
James Mayhew

Orion
Children's Books

ORION CHILDREN'S BOOKS

First published in Great Britain in 2016 by Hodder and Stoughton

2 4 6 8 10 9 7 5 3 1

Text and illustrations copyright © James Mayhew, 2016

A CIP catalogue record for this book
is available from the British Library.

ISBN 978 1 4440 1573 7

Printed and bound in China

The paper and board used in this book are from well-managed
forests and other responsible sources.

Orion Children's Books
An imprint of
Hachette Children's Group
Part of Hodder and Stoughton
Carmelite House
50 Victoria Embankment
London EC4Y 0DZ

An Hachette UK Company

www.hachette.co.uk
www.hachettechildrens.co.uk

In memory of
Levi Mayhew
– another brave boy hero –
J. M.

Contents

Chapter One

Long ago, in the days of knights and castles and magic, there lived a wizard.

His name was Merlin.

Merlin lived in a small house
in a dark forest.

The house was filled with books
and pots and jars full of potions,
and was very dusty because
Merlin never did any housework.

Instead, he spent his days reading
books and learning about magic.

But Merlin was worried.

All over Britain, battles were
being fought. All because there
was no king.

Ever since the old king had died,
no one could decide who should
be the next king.

Merlin thought it should be
someone kind and forgiving.

Not someone who wanted to
fight all the time.

He wanted the battles to stop.

Chapter Two

Most days, Merlin was kept busy teaching a young boy called Arthur who had been adopted by Sir Ector, an old knight.

Sir Ector was a good man.
He already had a boy of his
own called Kay.

One stormy night, Merlin had
appeared with the baby Arthur.

He thought Arthur would make
a fine little brother for Kay.

And so, Arthur grew up with Kay
and they were good friends
most of the time.

But sometimes they fought.
Kay would say, "One day I will
be a great knight, just like my
father. You will never be a knight.
You are not my real brother!
No one knows who your
father really was."

Arthur felt sad, he longed to be a
brave knight and have adventures.

Merlin smiled and watched and
waited.

Chapter Three

Merlin taught Arthur all sorts
of things.

Arthur learned the
ways of the
birds and
animals.

Merlin taught Arthur to be
brave and strong.

He also taught him to be kind.

Arthur was clever and
learned fast.

"Do you know who my real parents were?" asked Arthur one day.

"Yes," said Merlin. "But you must learn to be patient."

Time passed . . .

Years went by . . .

Arthur grew
taller and taller.

Meanwhile, battles across Britain went on. And there was still no king.

And so Merlin decided it was time for some magic.

One day, in a churchyard in
London, Merlin cast a spell on
a sword. He pushed the magic
sword through a metal anvil
and into a big stone.
It was stuck!

But magic words appeared on
the stone.

They said: *Whoever pulls this
sword out of the stone is the true
King of England.*

Chapter Four

The story of the sword in the
stone spread far and wide.

Merlin laughed as he watched all the big and brave knights trying to pull the sword out.

None of them could do it.
So the knights decided to have a
competition on New Year's Day.

The news soon reached Sir Ector's house. Young Kay wanted to enter.

He had always dreamed of being a knight in shining armour, and this was his chance. He asked Arthur to look after his armour and sword.

Sir Ector, Kay and Arthur set
off for London. It was a long
journey, but when they arrived
everyone was very excited.

As he was getting ready, Kay realised he had forgotten his sword. "This is your fault," he said to Arthur. "You should be looking after it!"

"Sorry," said Arthur. "I'll go and get it."

But there wasn't time to go all
the way home . . .

Chapter Five

Arthur ran around London Town,
trying to find somewhere to buy
or borrow a sword. But all the
shops were closed. Kay would
be so angry.

He had almost given up hope when he saw a sword! It was in a churchyard, pushed into an anvil and stone.

"Maybe that will do!" he thought.

He ran to the sword and took
hold of it.

With one pull, the sword slid
gently out of the stone. The blade
gleamed in the winter sunshine.

Young Arthur carried the sword all
the way back and gave it to Kay.
Kay knew it was the famous
sword at once.

"Look, Father," he said to Sir Ector.
"I have the Sword in the Stone! I
shall be king!"

"And did **YOU** pull the sword out of the stone?" asked Sir Ector.

Kay thought for a moment. Then he said, "No, Father . . . it was Arthur."

No one could believe a boy like
Arthur could have pulled the
sword from the stone.

Sir Ector and the knights went to
the churchyard and put the sword
back.

Then some of the knights tried to
pull it out. Even Kay tried.

But once again, the sword
was stuck.

Chapter Six

"Now then, Arthur, tell us, how did you pull the sword out?" asked Sir Ector.

"It was easy," said Arthur. "I just pulled . . . like this!"
All the knights kneeled down.
Arthur could not understand why.

And then, in a blaze of light,
Merlin appeared.

"Arthur," he said gently, "Your
true father was a king, and your
mother was a princess.

But I knew you were not safe,
because there were so many
battles around their castle. So I
took you to live with Sir Ector
until the time was right for
you to be king.

"And that time is now."

He turned to the knights
and said. "Here before you
stands your true king – Arthur
Pendragon!" Everyone cheered.
Britain had a new king.
Perhaps now there would be
no more battles.

Merlin returned to his little house
in the forest.

At last he could rest, knowing
that King Arthur would be a
good and kind king.

Just as he had taught him to be.